PINGU

the Doctor

BBC CHILDREN'S BOOKS

Pinga was in hospital with a broken arm. Pingu and Mum were on their way to visit her. As they approached the hospital entrance, an ambulance whizzed past.

"That penguin doesn't look too well," said Mum, shaking her head.

At the reception desk, Mum asked for Pinga. The nurse behind the desk looked Pinga's name up in a book to find out which room she was in.

Pingu stared at everything around him and began to feel uncomfortable. He didn't like the look of the wheelchairs and crutches one bit.

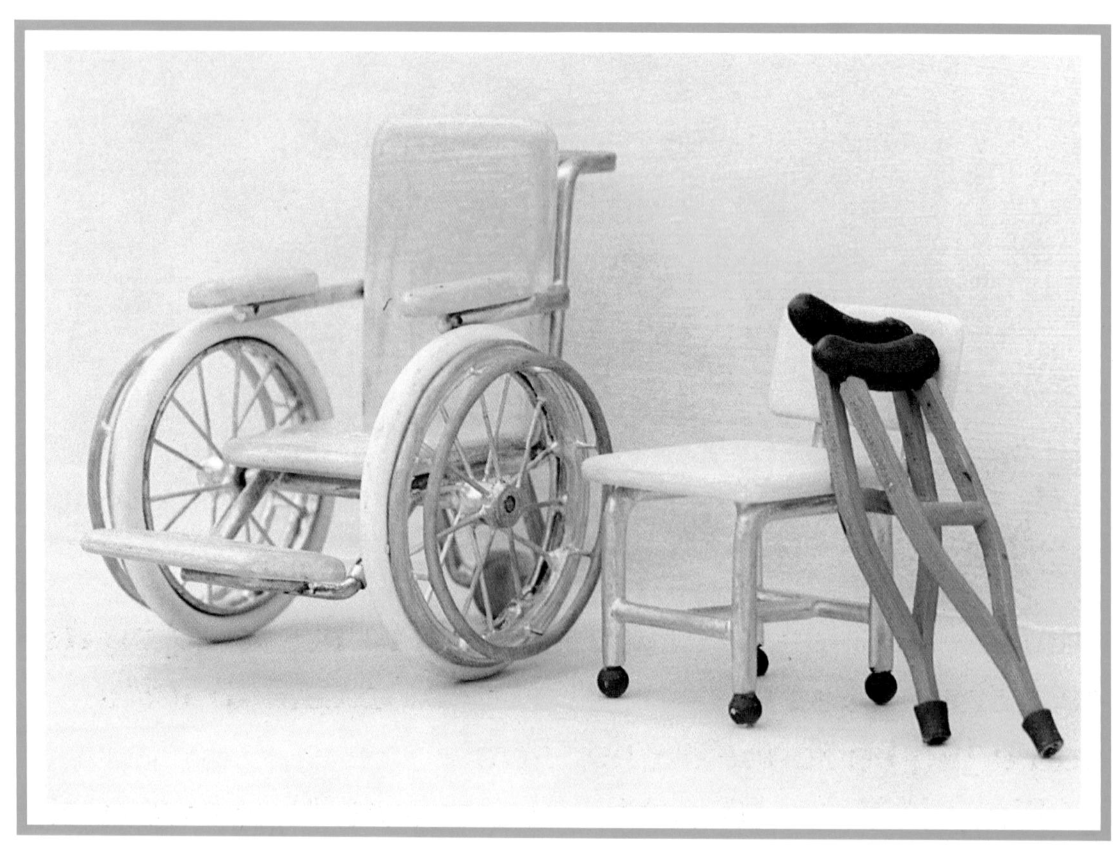

Pingu was very relieved to find Pinga sitting up in bed. She looked the same as usual except that she had a big bandage on her arm.

"Pinga!" he cried out in excitement. "Here we are!"

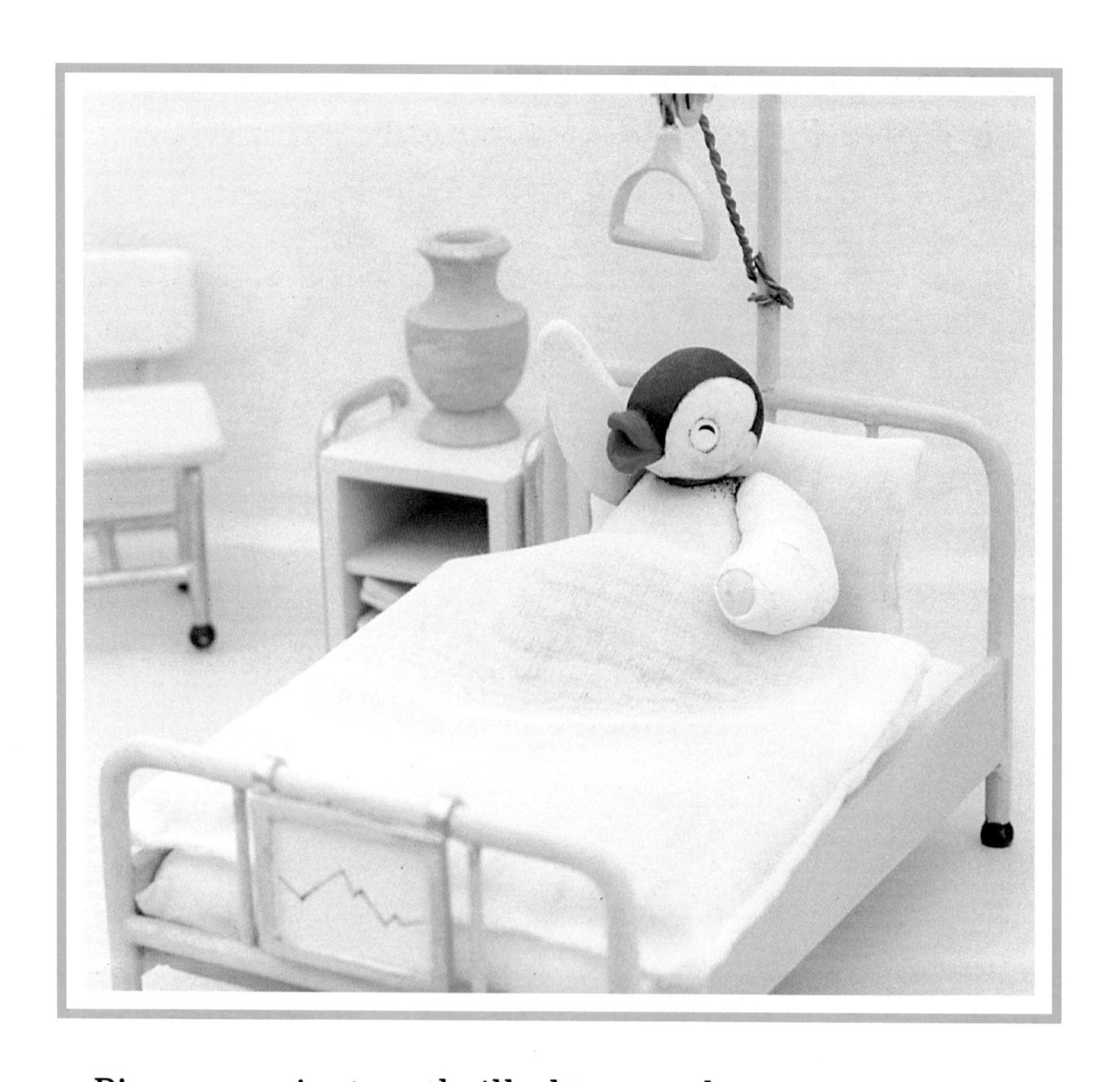

Pinga was just as thrilled to see them.
"Hurray!" she shouted out. "You've come at last. It's so boring just sitting here all day."

Mum patted Pinga on the head.

"My poor Pinga," she said, soothingly. "I hope your arm doesn't hurt too much."

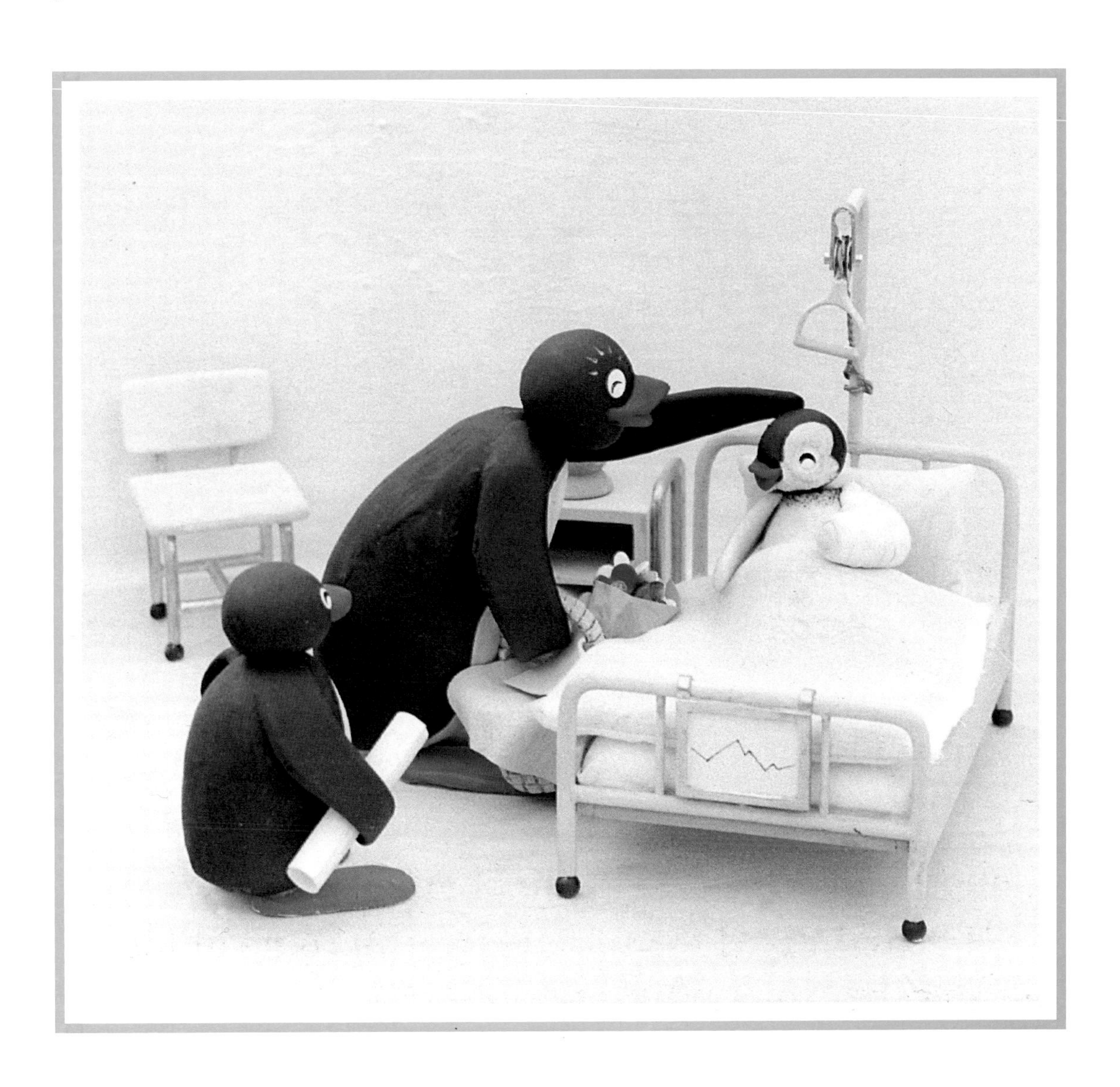

Pingu had drawn a picture of Pinga falling off the table breaking her arm. He held it up for Pinga to see and they all laughed about it.

In the next bed was a penguin who had broken her foot. The nurse came in to examine her.

"And how are you feeling today?" asked the nurse as she peered into the penguin's mouth.

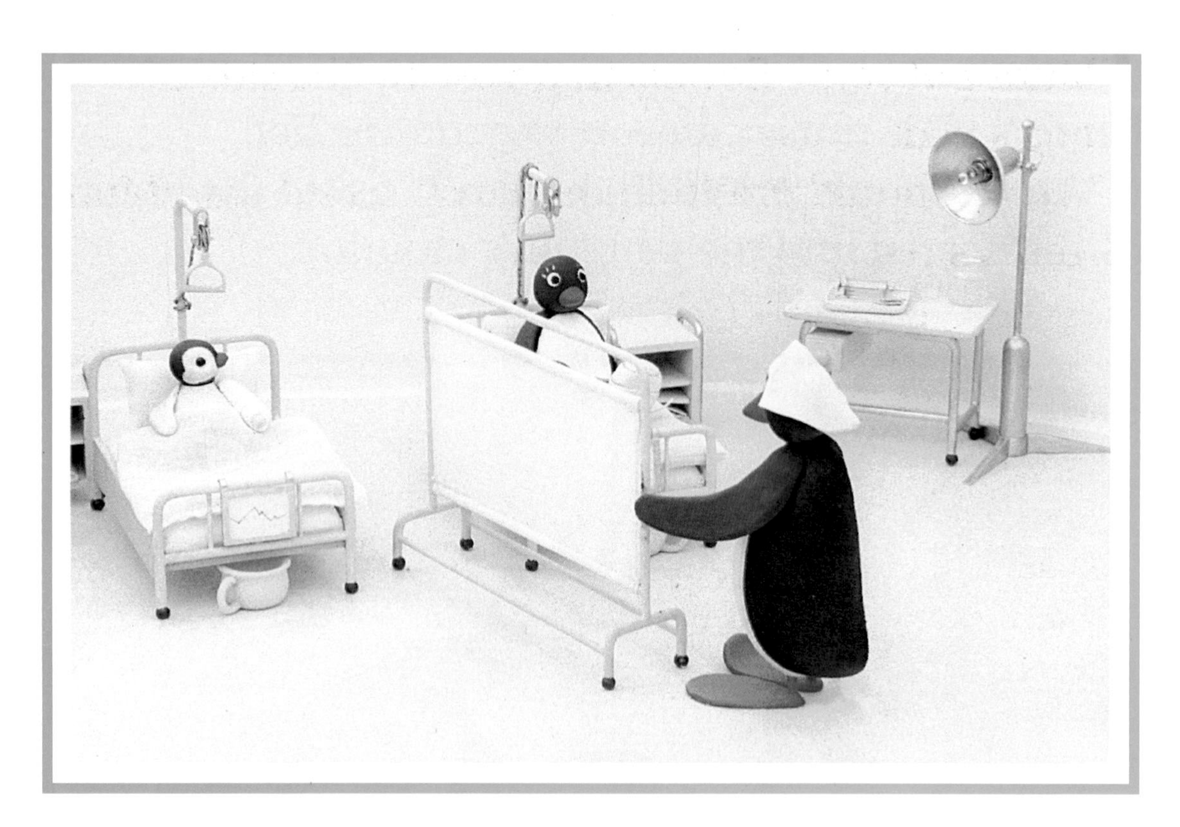

"I'll have a look at your foot now," said the nurse.

She moved a large screen over to hide the patient's bed. Mum and Pingu looked rather alarmed.

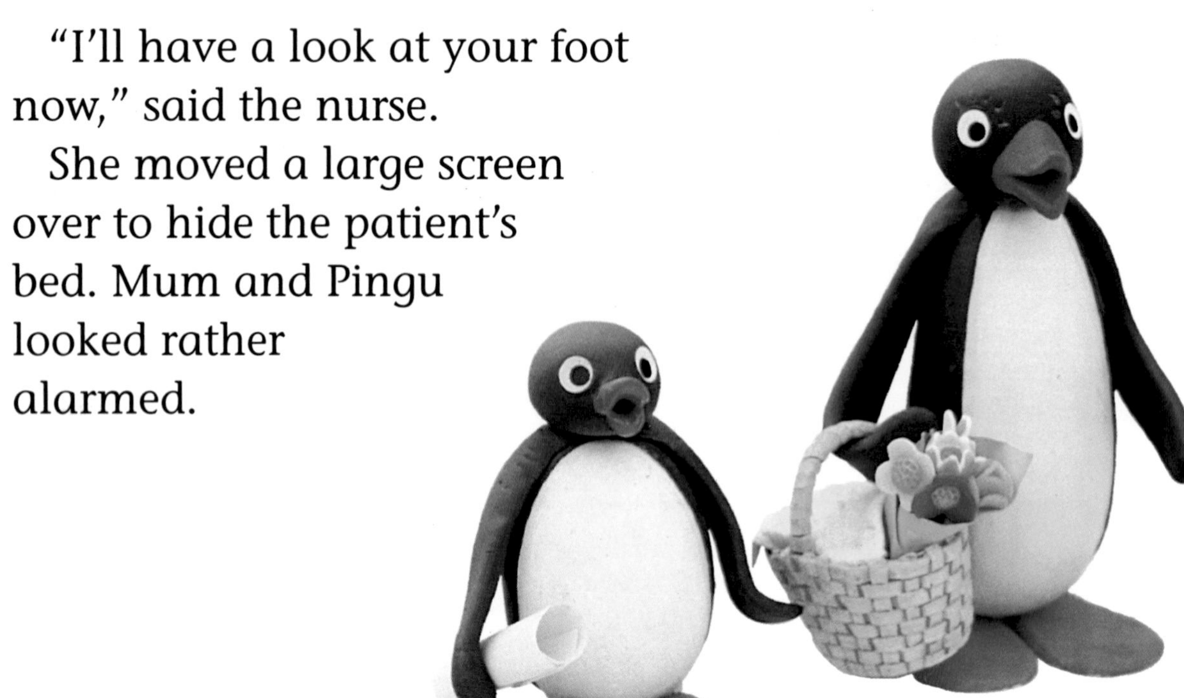

Mum put some flowers in a vase by the side of Pinga's bed.

"These should brighten things up a bit," said Mum cheerfully.

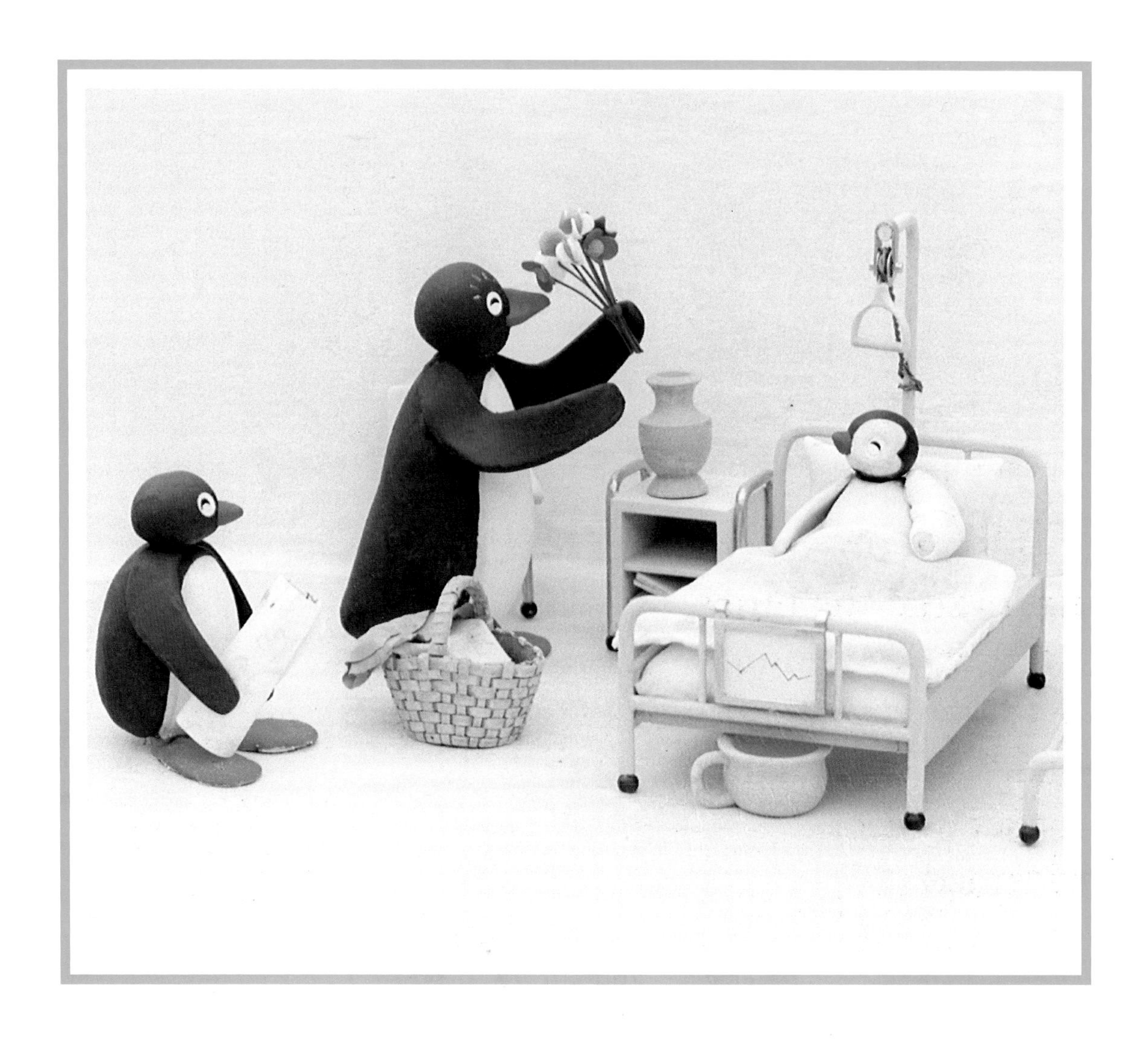

“I want to come home, Mum,” said Pinga. “I miss you.”

“And I miss you too, little Pinga,” said Mum, giving her a big kiss. “You’ll be better very soon and then you can come home.”

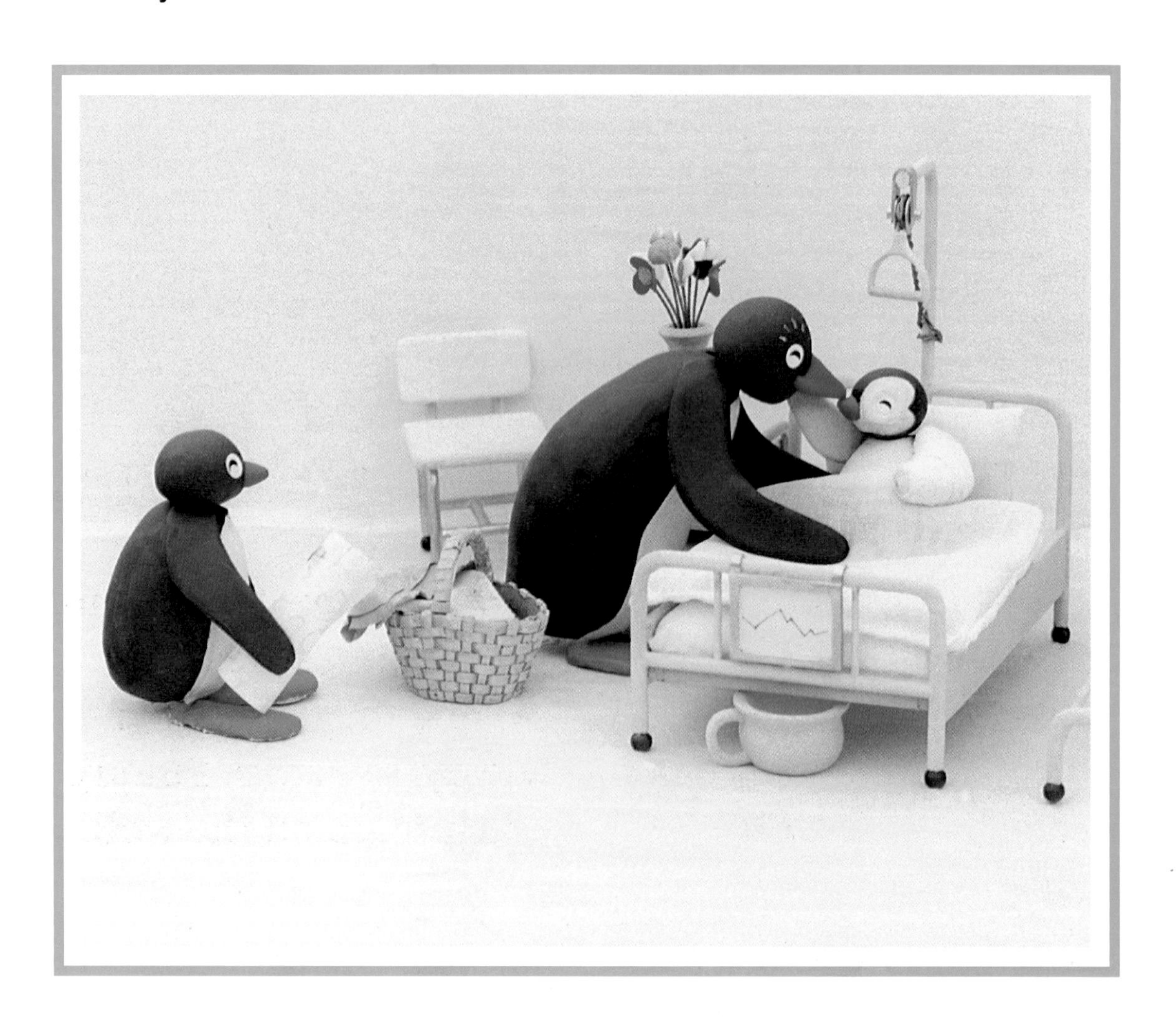

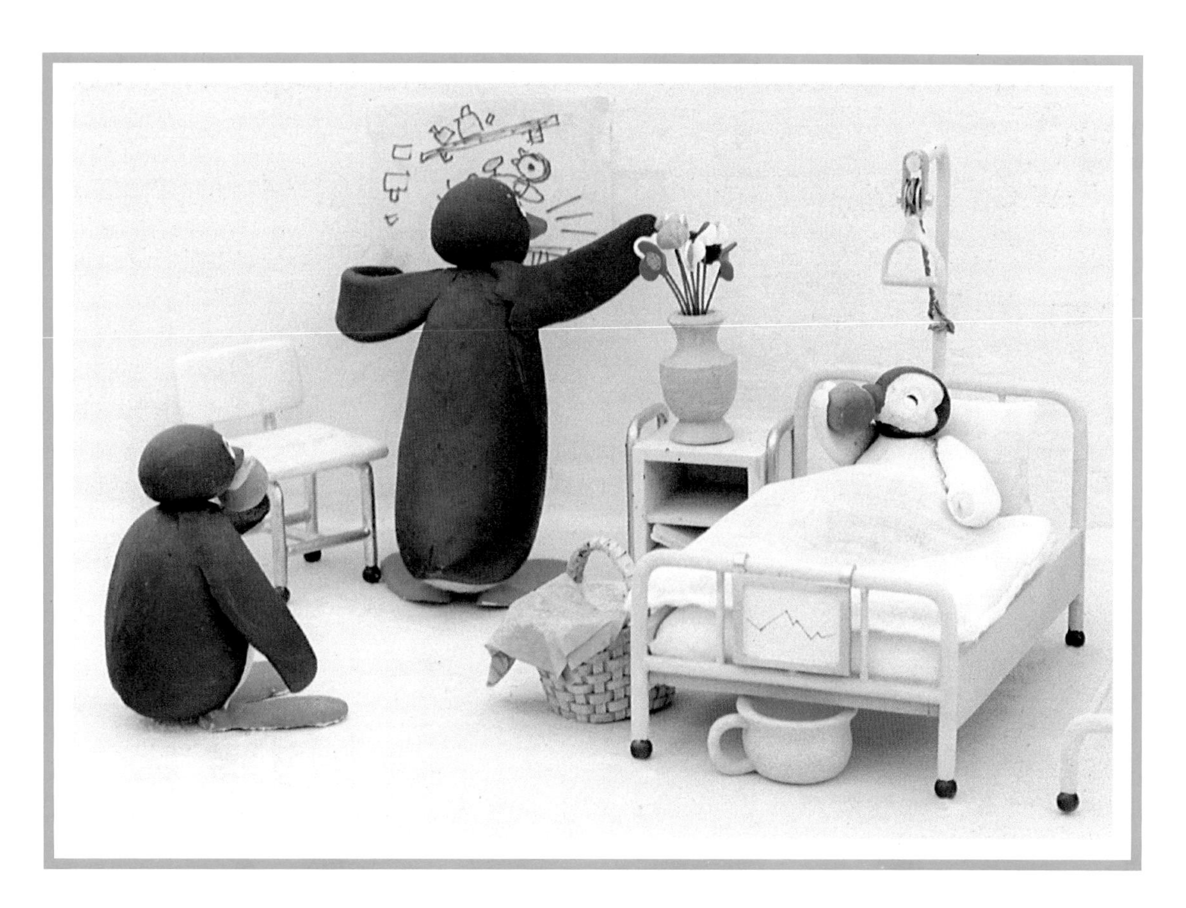

Mum gave Pingu and Pinga an apple each. While they crunched away, she stuck Pingu's picture up on the wall.

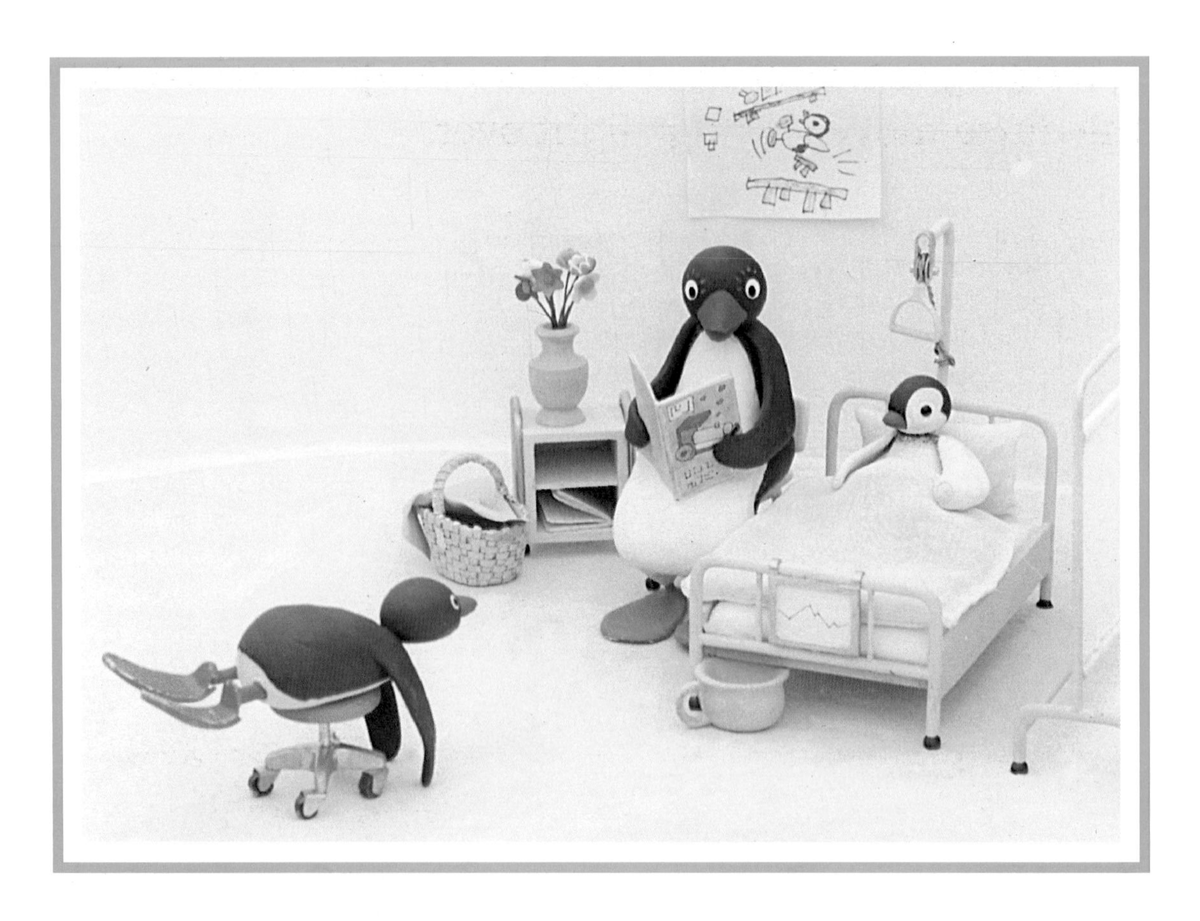

The time passed slowly. Mum read a long story to Pinga. Pingu pushed himself round and round the room on a chair with wheels.

"I'm going to have to find a way to liven things up a bit," he thought to himself.

Looking across at the next bed, Pingu watched as the nurse moved a huge light over.

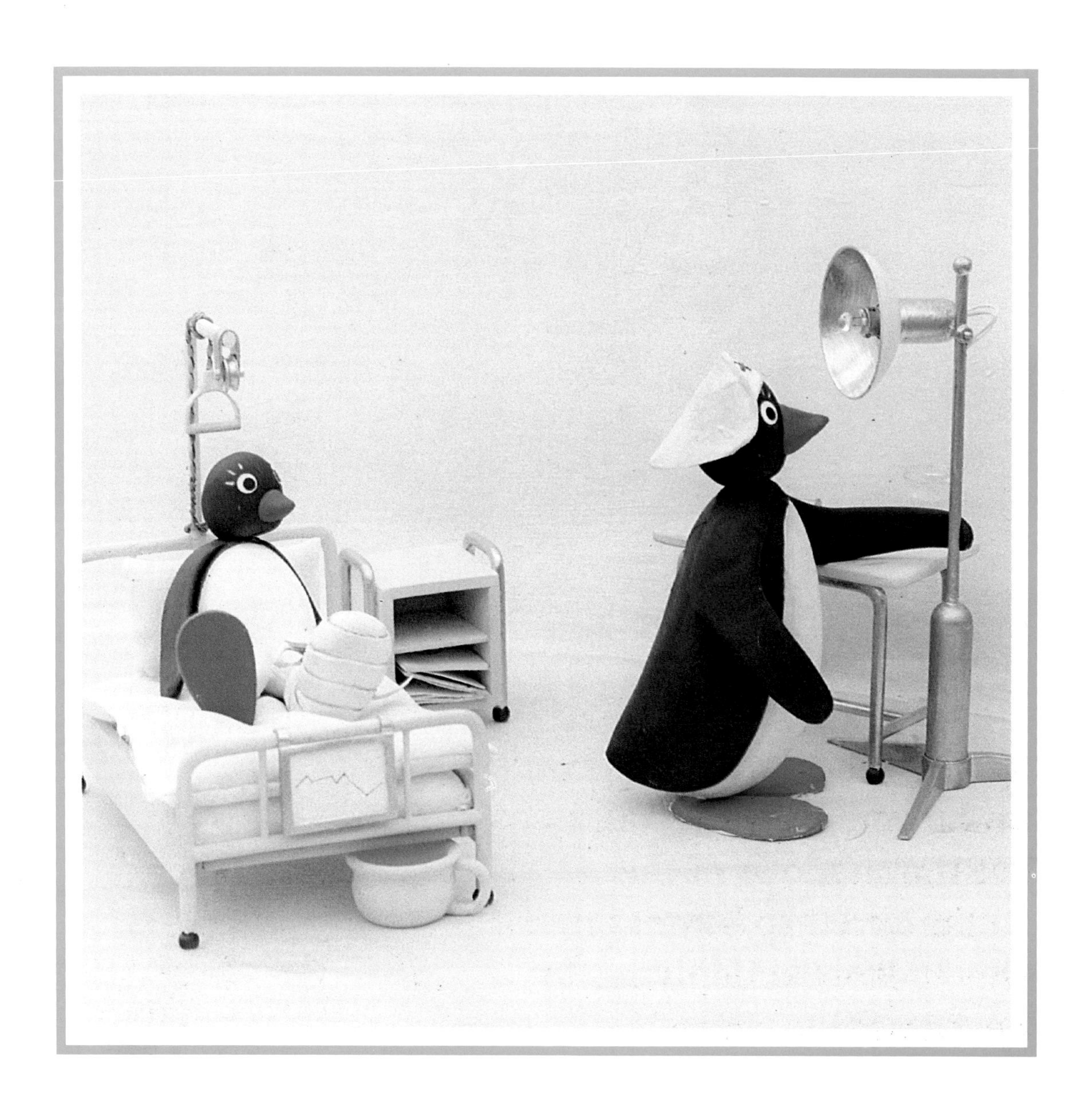

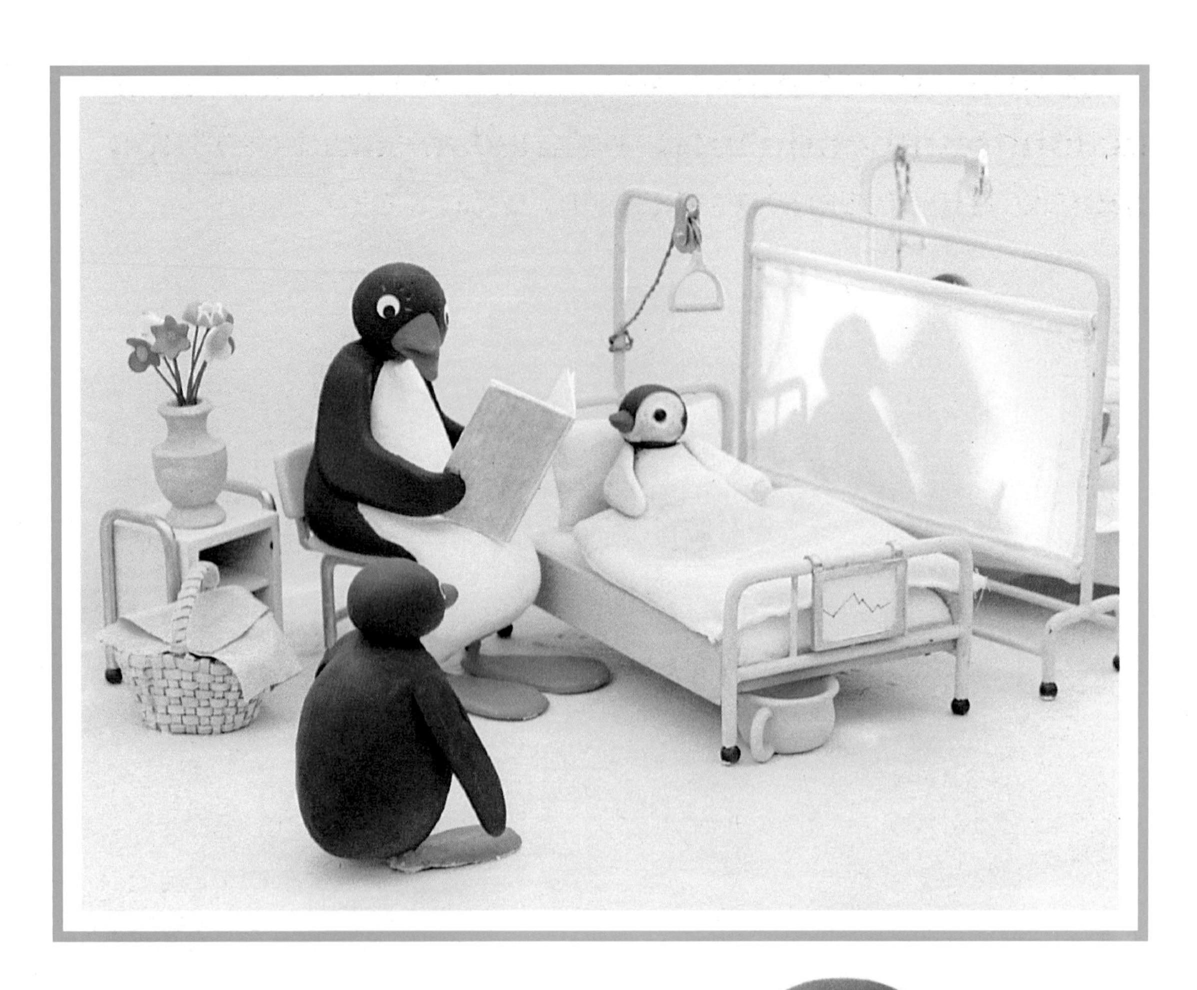

When the light was switched on, Pingu could see the shadows of the nurse and the patient on the screen. Suddenly he had an idea.

As soon as the nurse had gone, Pingu swept into action. Mum and Pinga watched amazed as Pingu moved the screen in front of Pinga's bed.

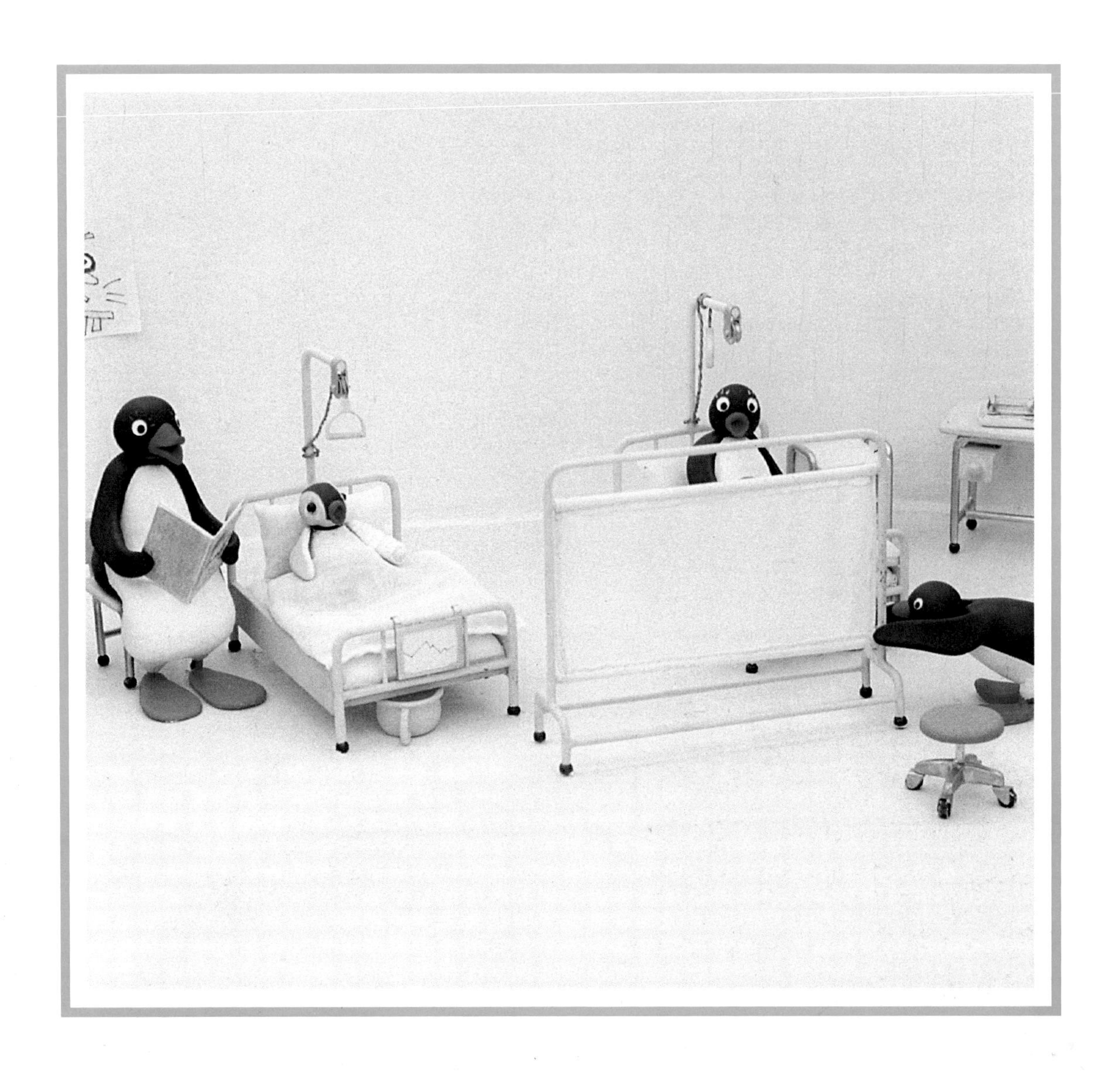

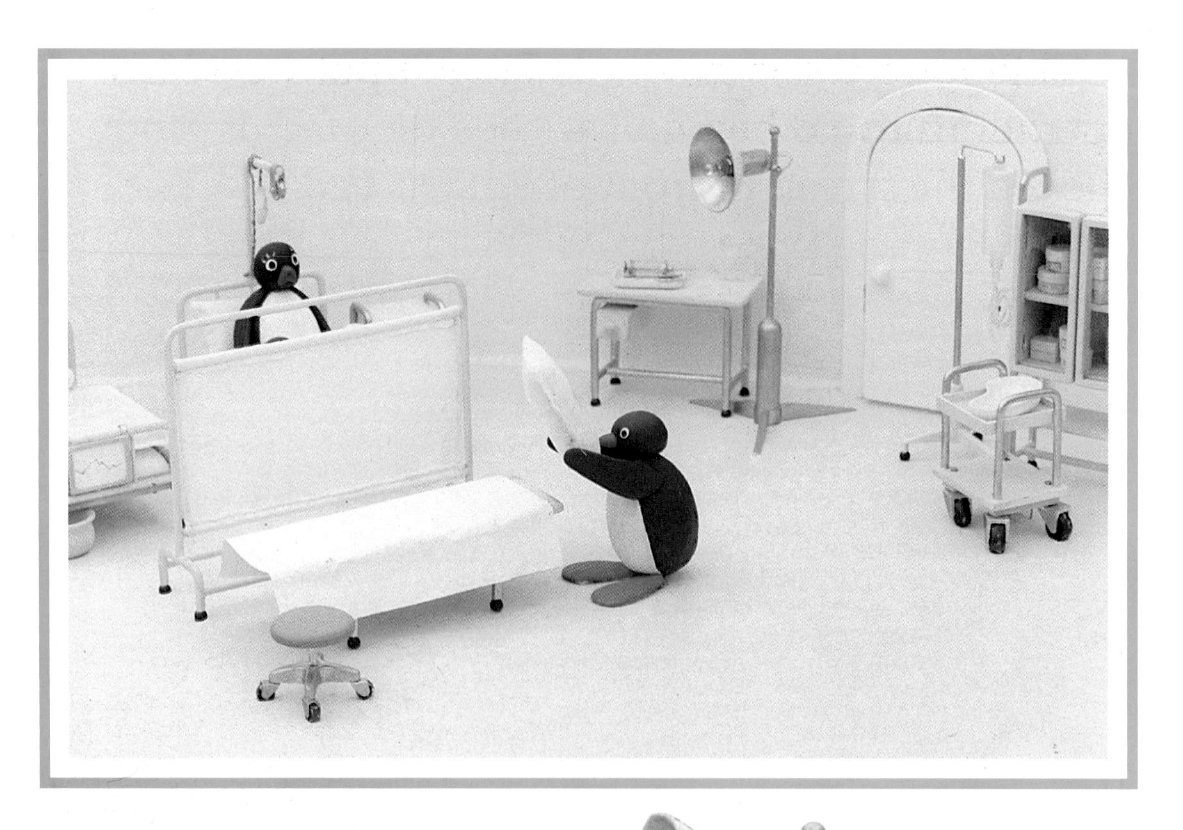

Behind the screen he placed a bed with a pillow on it. Then he moved the big light across the room. The other little penguin wondered what was going on.

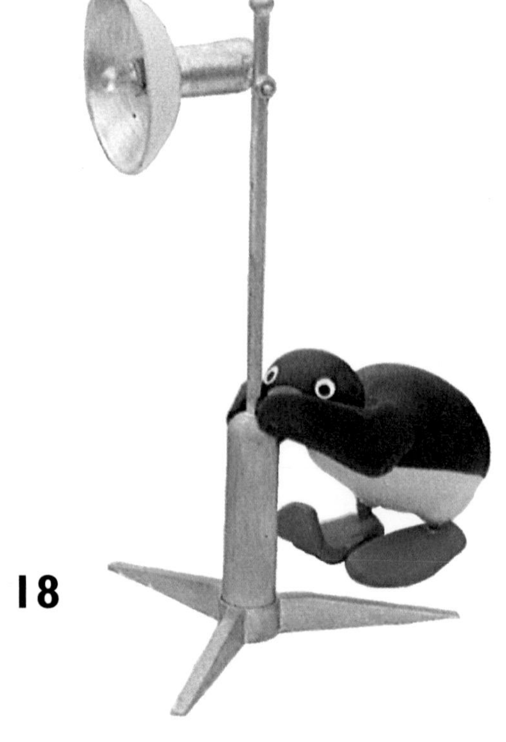

All Pingu needed now was Pinga's potty and his operations could begin.

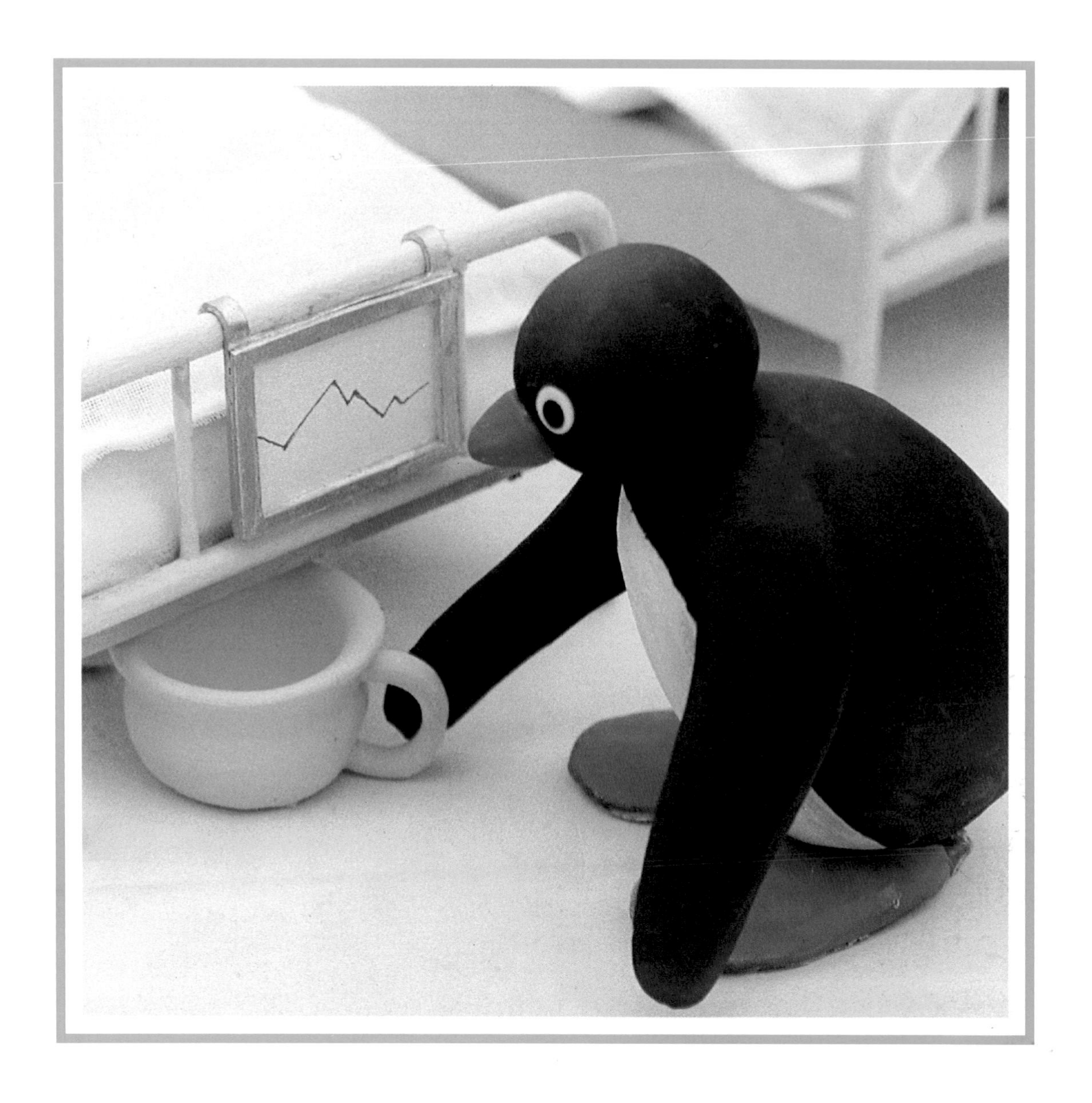

Suddenly Mum and Pinga realised what was happening. Looking at the screen, they saw the shadow of a patient on a bed with Doctor Pingu standing beside him. They began to chuckle.

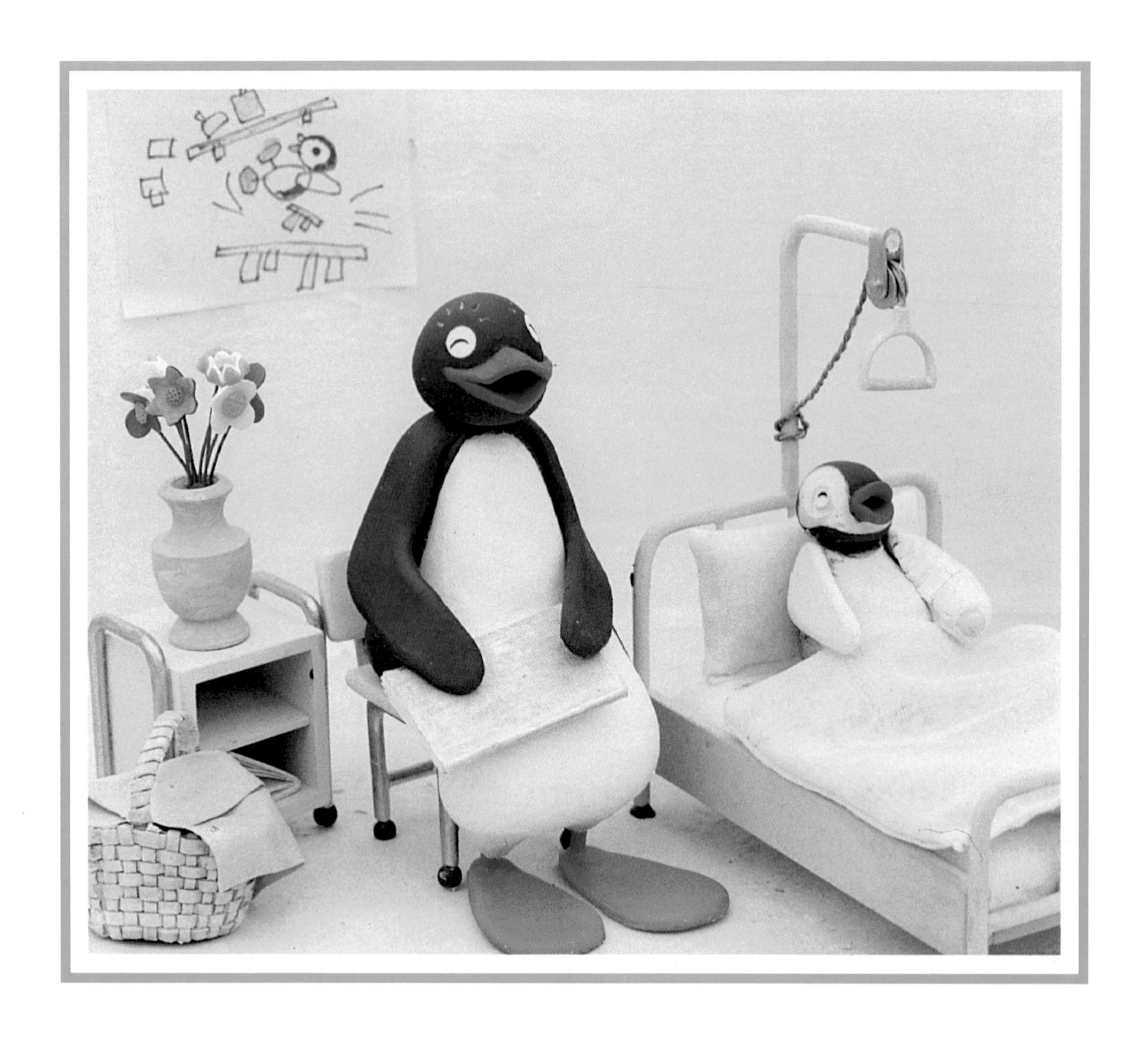

First, Doctor Pingu examined his patient with a stethoscope.

"Things don't sound too good," he exclaimed to himself as he listened.

With a great flourish, Doctor Pingu produced a huge pair of scissors and began to cut open the patient's tummy. Snip, snip, snip.

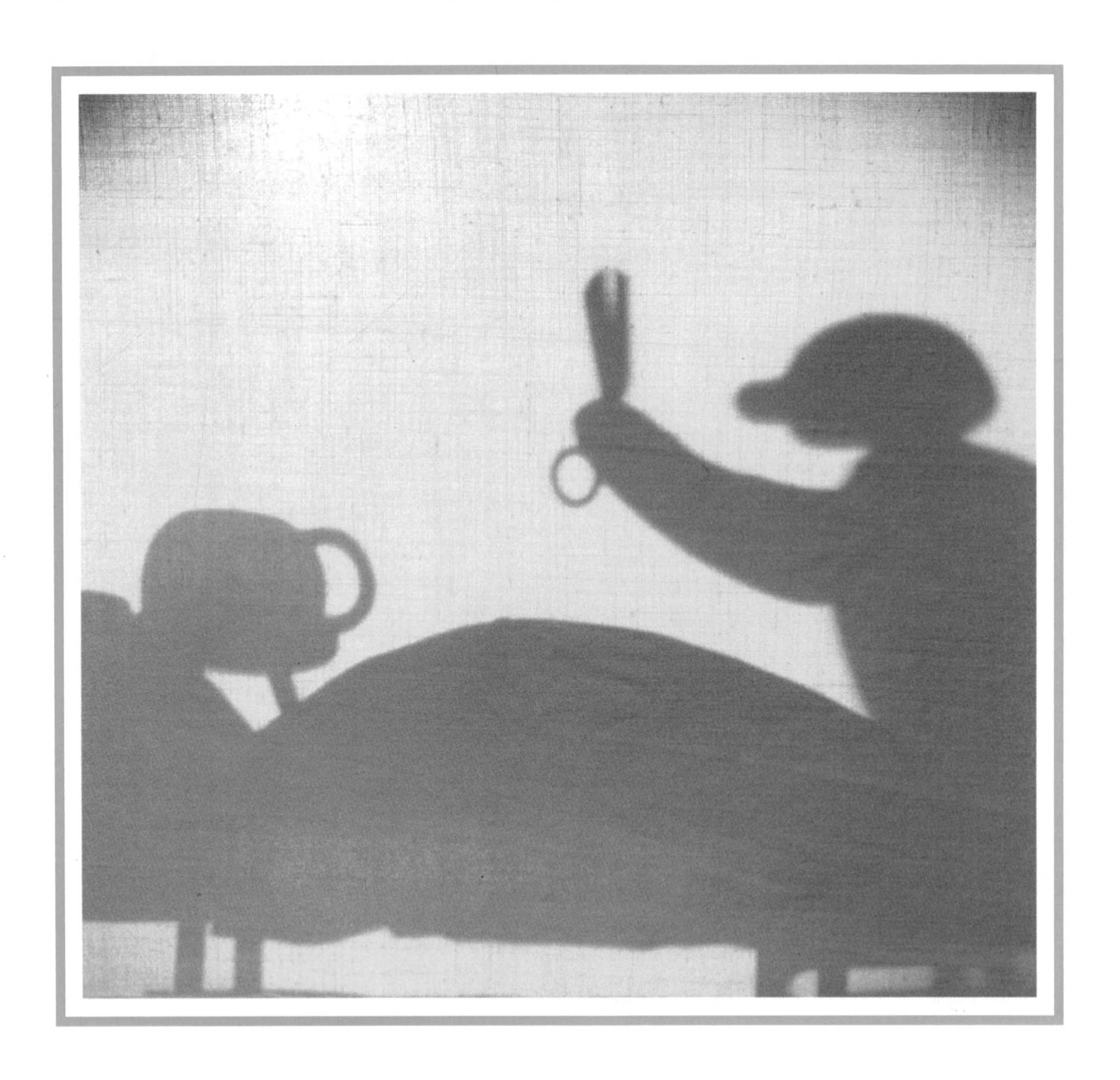

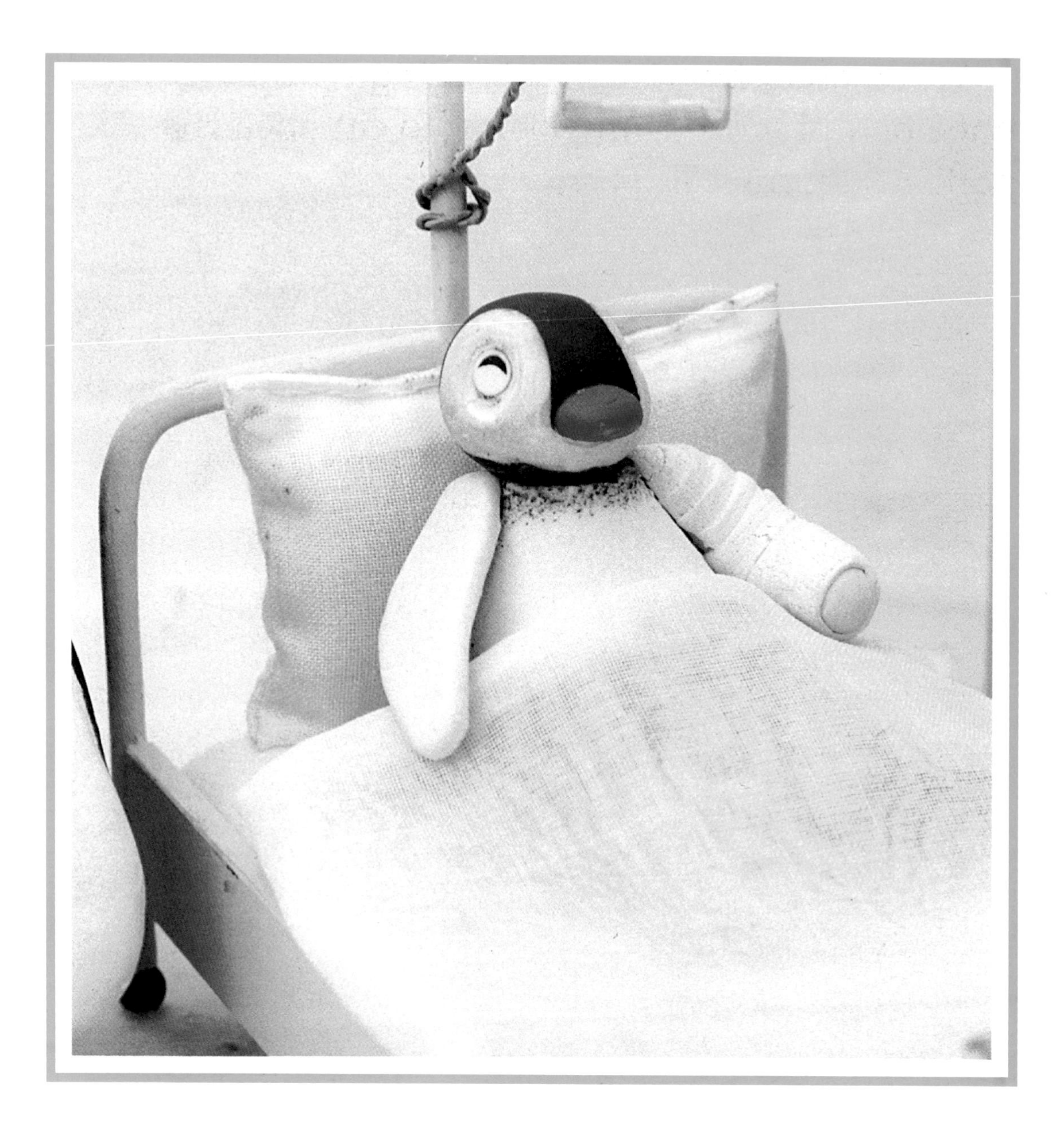

Pinga hooted with laughter.

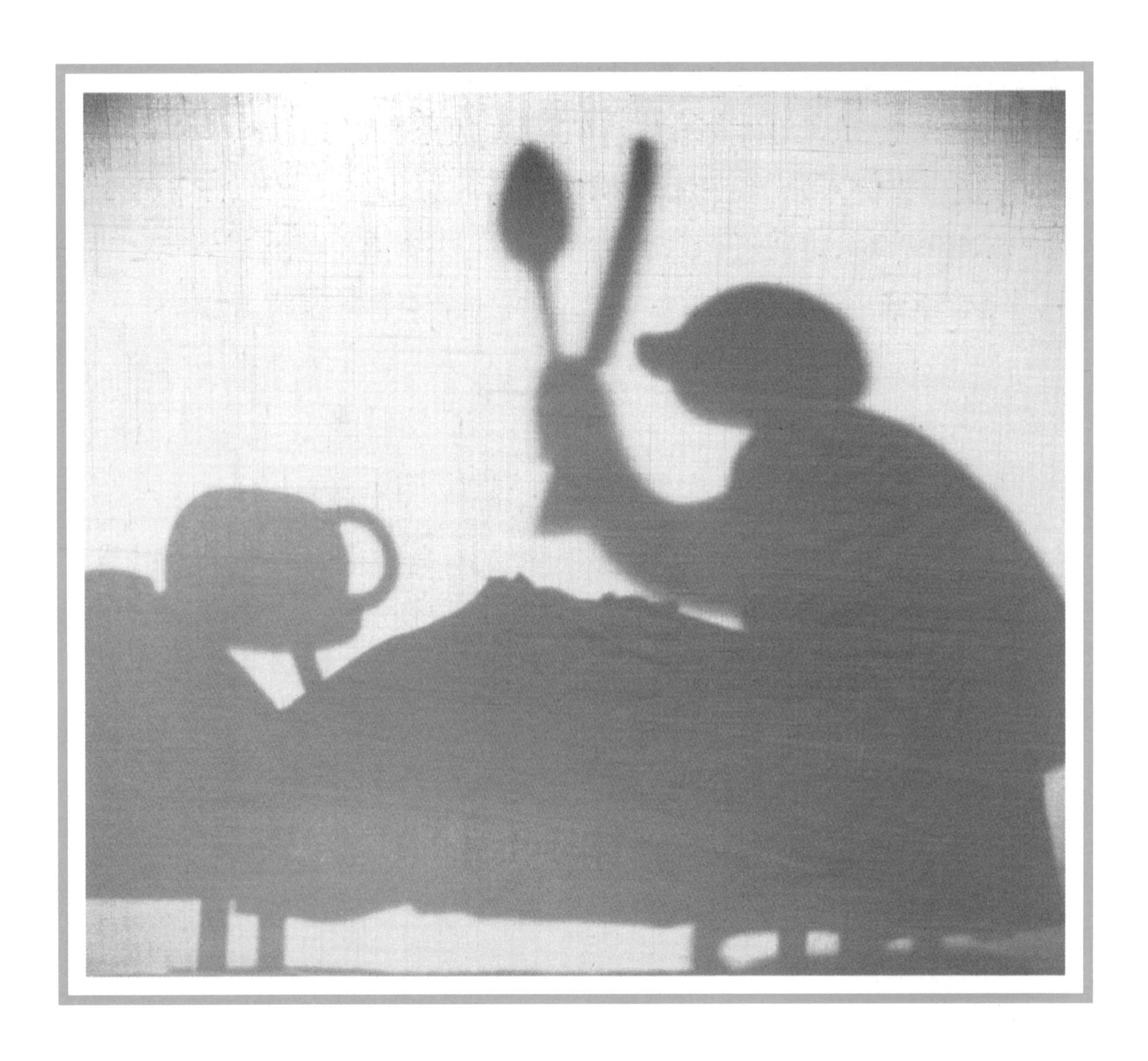

Out of the patient's stomach Doctor Pingu pulled a hot-water bottle, a long piece of string and then, finally, a large spoon and a knife.

"Dear, dear," he muttered to himself.

Pinga, Mum and the other little penguin were laughing so loudly that a nurse and a doctor standing outside the door heard all the commotion.

"What on earth is going on in there?" they asked each other.

The nurse and the doctor came into the room just as Pingu was sewing up his patient's stomach.

Behind the screen, Pingu was sewing up the sheet with huge, clumsy stitches. Suddenly, he heard some different voices laughing in the room.

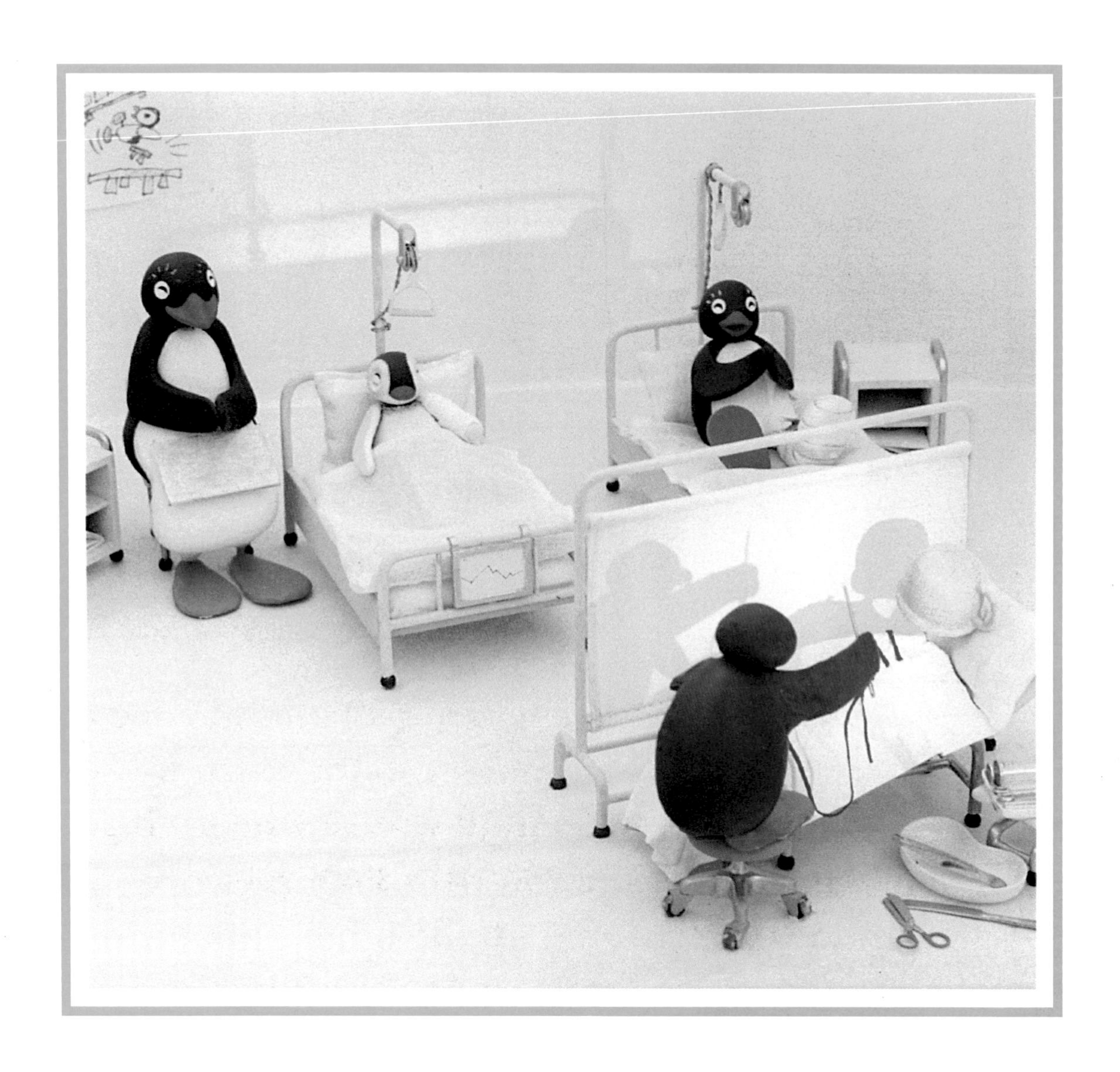

It was the nurse and doctor.

"Bravo!" they shouted. "You're doing fine work, Doctor. And you've cheered up the other patients as well," they added, looking at Pinga's smiling face.

Pingu popped his head round the screen and grinned at everyone.

"The show is over!" he announced.

"I think you should try on a real doctor's outfit now," said the doctor. So while Pingu stood on a stool, the doctor dressed him in an operating mask and hat and placed a stethoscope round his neck.

“All set for the operating theatre, Doctor Pingu?” asked the nurse, and everyone laughed. They’d had fun in hospital after all.

Other PINGU books available from BBC Children's Books:

Pingu and the Birthday Present
Pingu and the Broken Toys
Pingu Celebrates Christmas
Pingu the Chef
Pingu and the Circus
Pingu and the Kite
Pingu Looks After the Egg
Pingu and the Messy Meal
Pingu and the New Baby
Pingu and the Spotty Day
Pingu and Pinga Stay Up

Pingu the Postman Wheelie Book
Pingu Lift-the-Flap Book

Fun with Pingu Activity Book
Fun with Pingu Christmas Activity Book
Fun with Pingu Colouring Book
Fun with Pingu Press-Out and Story Book
Fun with Pingu Sticker and Story Book

Pingu Mini Books
Pingu Chunky Books

Published by BBC Children's Books
a division of BBC Worldwide Limited
Woodlands, 80 Wood Lane, London W12 0TT
First published 1996

ISBN 0 563 40440 X

Typeset by BBC Children's Books
Colour separations by DOT Gradations, Chelmsford
Printed and bound by Cambus Litho, East Kilbride